The
BOY
and the
BEAR

by
Peter Stein

Holiday House New York

Copyright © 2019 by Peter Stein
All Rights Reserved
HOLIDAY HOUSE is registered in the U.S. Patent and Trademark Office.
Printed and bound in January 2019 at Toppan Leefung, DongGuan City, China.
The artwork was created with graphite and digital color.
www.holidayhouse.com
First Edition
1 3 5 7 9 10 8 6 4 2

Library of Congress Cataloging-in-Publication Data
Names: Stein, Peter (Peter Lawrence), author, illustrator.
Title: The boy and the bear / Peter Stein.
Description: First edition. | New York : Holiday House, [2019] |
Summary: A boy experiences the gamut of emotions when he loses
his beloved Teddy bear, then finds it again.
Identifiers: LCCN 2018024182 | ISBN 9780823440955 (hardcover)
Subjects: | CYAC: Stories in rhyme. | Teddy bears--Fiction. | Lost and found
        possessions—Fiction. | Emotions--Fiction.
    Classification: LCC PZ8.3.S8193 Bo 2019 | DDC [E]—dc23 LC record available
        at https://lccn.loc.gov/2018024182

For Lisa

A BIG THANK-YOU TO LORI, GABRIEL, ELIAS,
PAUL, JAN, TERI, ERIC, ANNA, AND ELIJAH.

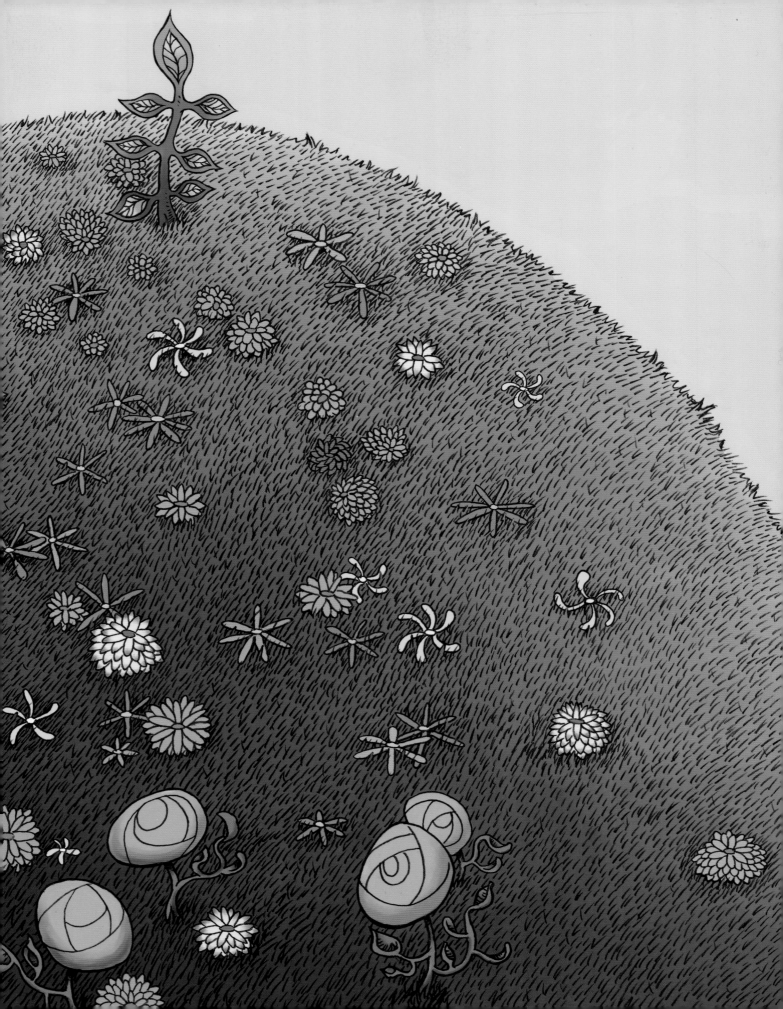

A boy had a bear.
A fuzzy brown bear.

It went with him here

and went with him  there.

The boy. The bear.

Always a pair.

And then one day . . .

The boy found a goat.
A potbellied goat in a polka-dot coat.

The goat in the coat
and the fuzzy brown bear
went with him here
and went with him there.

The boy found a slug.

A squishable, huggable, lovable slug.

The huggable slug,
the goat in the coat,
and the fuzzy brown bear
went with him here
and went with him there.

The boy found a monkey.

A funky old monkey.

The funky old monkey,
the huggable slug,
the goat in the coat,
and the fuzzy brown bear

went with him here
and went with him there.

The boy found a rat.
A rodeo rat in a ten-gallon hat.

The rodeo rat,
the funky old monkey,
the huggable slug,
the goat in the coat,
and the fuzzy brown bear
went with him here
and went with him there.

The boy found a thing.
He pulled on the string.
It started to sing.

Tra-la-la!

The sing-along thing,
the rodeo rat,
the funky old monkey,
the huggable slug,
the goat in the coat,
and the fuzzy brown bear

went with him here
and went with him there.

The boy found an otter.

Uh-oh.

First came a teeter,

then came a totter.

Suddenly—WHOA!

The boy shouted, "NO!"

The tottering otter,
the sing-along thing,
the rodeo rat,
the funky old monkey,
the huggable slug,
the goat in the coat,
and the fuzzy brown bear

flew in the air.

"Bear?" said the boy.
Where was the bear?

He wasn't down here.

Or way over there.

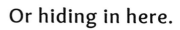

Or hiding in here.

Or ANYWHERE.

None of the others could ever compare.

"Where ARE you?" he cried.

"I WANT MY
BROWN BEAR!"

The bear found his boy.
The boy found his friend.
His fuzzy brown, lost and found,
very best friend.

And then . . .

The boy saw a blimp.
A delivery blimp
with a runaway shrimp
and a hog and a snail
and a frog and a whale
and a lamb and a moose
and a ram and a goose
plus MORE that he found
all scattered around.

A slippery latch had opened the hatch!

He knew what to do.

He threw . . .

and he threw . . .

and he threw . . .

and he THREW!

And then once again,
the boy and the bear
were simply a pair.

Everywhere.

FEELINGS

Sad   Happy   Angry

The boy felt so much in so many places.
Can you match the feelings with each of the faces?

Loving   Worried   Calm